This book belongs to...

_____

_____

_____

CITY OF COVENTRY LIBRARIES

WITHDRAWN

FOR SALE

3 8002 02423 545 1

D1077131

I, Pod

An original story by author Rebecca Lisle
© Rebecca Lisle
Illustrated by Richard Watson

MAVERICK ARTS PUBLISHING LTD
Studio 3A, City Business Centre, 6 Brighton Road, Horsham,
West Sussex, RH13 5BB, +44 (0)1403 256941
© Maverick Arts Publishing Limited
Published April 2019

A CIP catalogue record for this book
is available at the British Library.

ISBN 978-1-84886-406-1

www.maverickbooks.co.uk

Coventry City Council	
STO	
3 8002 02423 545 1	
Askews & Holts	May-2019
	£7.99

I, Pod

written by
Rebecca Lisle

illustrated by
Richard Watson

"Nim's a doddle to babysit," said Nim's

"She's very clever, she's learning to

"Hello

"My n

num.

alk already."

m," Pod said.

e is Pod."

Nim grinned.
"Pop!" she said.

Nim's mum smiled. "See? Brilliant!" And off she went.

"Can you say Pod?"
he asked the baby.

"Pot," Nim said.

Pod pointed, "That's
a pot," he said.

He pointed at Nim.
"You **Nim**," he said.

He tapped his chest:
"**I, Pod. I, Pod.**"

"**Pok**," said the baby.

"Pod," said Pod.

"Pol," said Nim.

Pod worked with stone, wood and vines to make a swing. Little Mammoth helped.

"Whee!" Nim cried.

Pod swung her harder and **higher** and **higher**...

It sailed over the rocks, over the trees and fell **PLOP** into the river.

"Poor little Nim!" Pod cried. "I'm coming! I'll get you!"

"Watch out! That's a terrible green snapper!"
The massive fish tried to snatch her -

"Snap! Snap!" said Nim.

Whoosh went the river, sweeping the baby away.

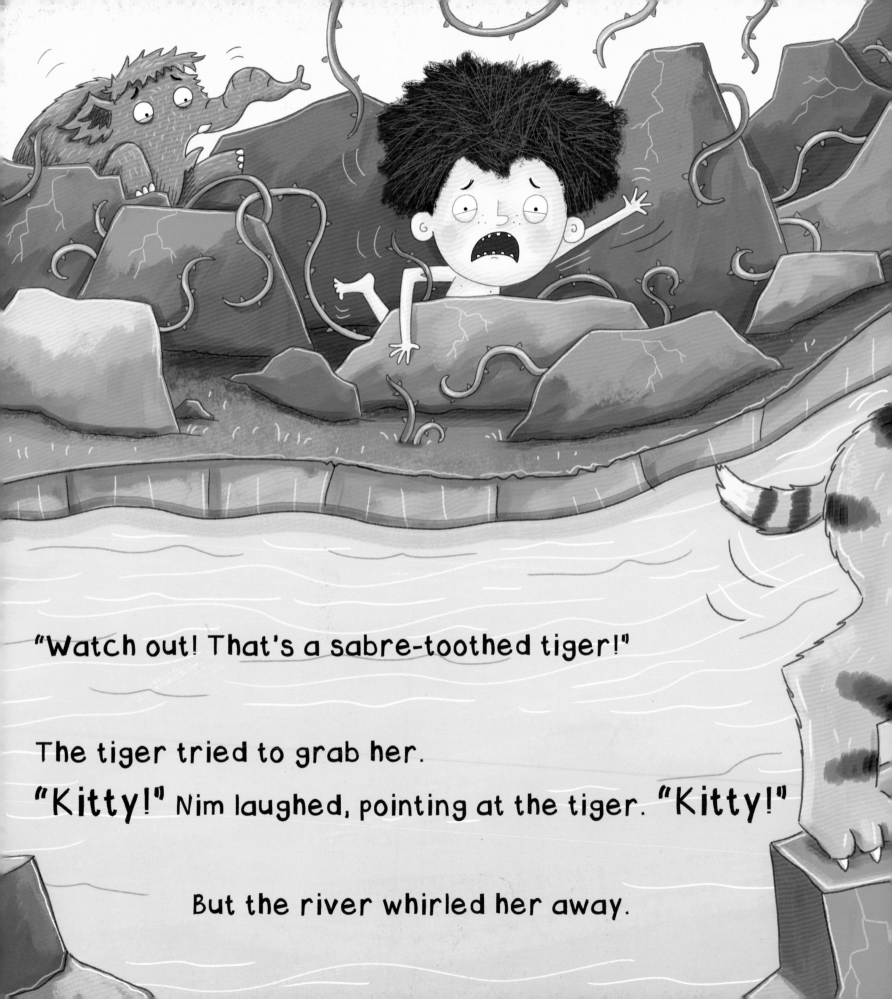

"Watch out! That's a sabre-toothed tiger!"

The tiger tried to grab her.

"Kitty!" Nim laughed, pointing at the tiger. "Kitty!"

But the river whirled her away.

"Watch out!" Pod cried, as a huge bird swooped down.

"That's a big beaky eagle!"

Nim chuckled. "Chick-chick!" she said.

But the river twirled her away.

...Little Mammoth thundered past and ran straight at a tree...

Whoomp

It toppled over.

Pod ran across the fallen tree. He scooped Nim up.

"Got you!"

Nim was wet. Pod was wet.

"Thank you, Little Mammoth!" said Pod.

"Now let's go home, Nim."

"Oh gracious me!" Nim's mum cried. "What happened? Where's her rattle? Her blanket? Her bonnet?"

Pod stared at his feet. How could he explain?

A tornado? A hurricane? An earthquake? A flood?

Before Pod could speak, Nim's mum said,
"**Who** did this, Nim?"

Nim pointed at Pod.

"Pod!

The End